The Fireflies are helping,
leaving twinkles all around,

For this festive happy season's
on its way, so no more frowns.

The magic's feeling different,
so much lighter, more relaxed,

The Pixies and the Fairies
much hard work has reached the max.

For now, it's time Jack Frost to
bear the load with watchful eyes,

It's the season of fair winter,
where there's snowball games and pies.

He lets the Fae and Pixies
take their well-earned winter rest,

Whilst he makes sure that nature
follows suit, doing his best.

He puts to sleep all nature
to help them renew, restore,

Ready for the spring when
life rejuvenates once more.

The peace on Earth prepares
with one last celebration first,

All the jolly laughs and merriment
seems near fit to burst.

Yule logs brought in rows around
the villages and homes,

Draped with berries, holly, *magic*
and some festive weather cones.

Decorated finely
with lots of love and smiley faces,

Gathering together
sprucing up all open spaces.

This time of year is
when they share,
all that they have
now gained.

The year that's past,
the cycle where
connections have been made.

Another time of growth,
many blessings
the Earth
has sowed.

There's offerings exchanged,
where thoughtful gifts
are now bestowed.

The smell of cinnamon
and chestnuts fill the forest air,

Everyone's all gathered
without worry nor troubled cares.

The party celebrations
go on all throughout the night,

Even the young stay up for once,
which is to their delight.

The Holly King is handing
the reigns to the Oak King,

As the darkest day is done, for now,
more light the day shall bring.

The passing of the seasons,
is a time for all to learn,

The lessons they all share,
are part of growth that's theirs to earn.

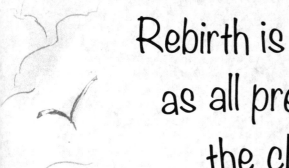

Rebirth is near;
as all prepare for
the changes that's in store,

Following the path of
Mother Earth
whose rhythm is the law.

Together in great harmony,
all life supports each other,

Rebalance is restored,
or else the Earth would surely suffer.

White Mistletoe unites
divine spirit upon the Earth,

Is hung around the village
and around each homely hearth.

Holly brought around the place,
brings lush green beauty closer,

Red berries let us know,
that life is ripe whilst it is colder.

Robins and their redbreasts
bringing messages from heaven,

Past loved ones give wisdom and *hope*
to those who care and miss them.

This ancient *festival*
brings loving peace and restoration,

Kindness and much time for rest,
all need a short vacation.

Berry and Wanda gifted
the lighting of the
Great Yule Log,

Each a candle to be lit
that is watched over by the
hedgehogs.

Because this year is quite unique,
as once two celebrations,

Now combined together,
Fae and Pixies have firm foundations.

Bringing the Great Yule Log with care
to wise old Salix Whisper,

All dance with merry tunes
around their happy, grounded sister.

The warmth of a strong fire pit
keeps everyone all snug,

Hearing tales of years gone by,
whilst sipping drinks from a hot mug.

A special time to gather
and to share each other's presence,

The memories resulting
are better than any presents.

The festive times of
Yuletide
start to drawn into a close,

As sunrise lends the morning light,
fair winters reign now grows.

The celebrations finished,
once again, it's come and gone,

Time for Pixies and the Fae
to take their rest, so now come on.

All make their way back to their homes,
their hearts all filled with glee,

So much magic all around,
A fine success, don't you agree?

The End

Making Mindful Memories

Late December can be such a special time for many of us where we can look forward to lots of lights, decorations, parties and maybe even presents.

Berry and Wanda know how good it can be to give as well as to receive. One way that we can do this is to think about how we can give back to others. Did you know that it doesn't have to be presents? There are lots of different ways in which we can help make others happy. It can also make us feel really good as well.

Making mindful memories can be the best gift that you can get because we carry them with us in our hearts.

What ways do you make mindful memories with you friends, family and people you care about?

Are there any things you can think of that you would like to do to make more mindful memories?

Remember making mindful memories doesn't have to wait until December; we can do it all year!

Magic Words:

I have some amazing mindful memories, and I am making more every day.